One Drop, Endless Ripples

By Jayshree L Patel

Illustrated by Alexandra McLellan

ISBN: 978-1-956364-00-2 (paperback) / 978-1-956364-01-9 (hardback) / 978-1-956364-02-6 (ebook)
Library of Congress Control Number: 2021916031

Illustrations by Alexandra McLellan.
Book design by Bryony van de Merwe.
Edited by Lisa A. Kramer.

Publisher: Ripple Press LLC

Visit the author's website: www.01drop.com

I am the river,
  flowing downstream,
    turning rocks into sand...
      One drop, endless ripples...

Jayshree L Patel

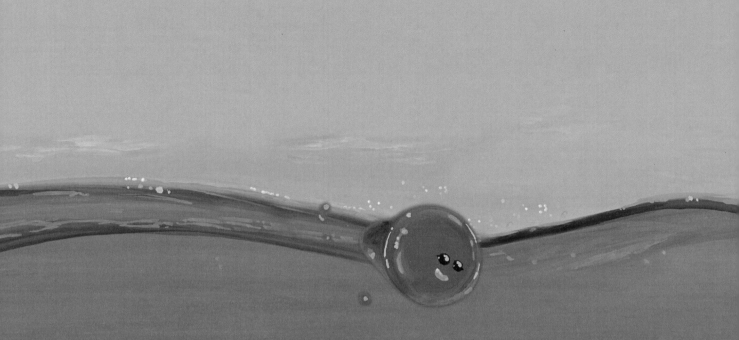

For my future grandchildren, including little Zeeyan, whose arrival sparked my book dream.
To Nihal and Anish, you are my biggest inspiration.
To Mum, Dad and Prakash, I am forever grateful for your unconditional love and support.
A special thanks to Lisa A. Kramer for helping me release my creative flow.

Jayshree

Thank you to Mom (Margaret) and Dad (Kevin). You have given me everything I have ever
needed to pursue my passion and I am so grateful for your support.

To my best friend and "art director", Lindsey. Thanks for listening to all my crazy ideas -
you always steer me in the right direction.

Alexandra

This book belongs to:

and is a gift from:

High in the sky.

Cocooned in the clouds.

One cold day.
"Brr!"
My cloud bursts open!

"Free!"

Flying!

Floating through the sky!

Down...

Down...

Down...

Landing softly ...
    Settling in my white bed.
              Blanket of snow.
                  Soft, still, sparkling snowflake.

One cold morning...

Glacial.

Shivering.

Shimmering.
Ice crystal.

Frozen still.

"What next?"

Floating, free, flowing.

Dancing downstream.

Riverbank amphitheater.

Trees and grass, bowing and swaying
to our wind song.

Resting in the spring pool.
Gleaming, gurgling.

Frolicking fish in my belly.
"Hee, hee, hee."

Swimming, shimmering, swirling.

Basking in the sunlight.

Basking in the moonlight.

Shimmering moon dancing on my belly.

"Ahh."

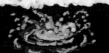

Diving, dipping, deep...
Down...
Down...
Down...
Exploring the mysterious world below.

Flowing, free. Floating downstream. Riding over rocks. Gliding over gravel.

My ebb and flow, turning rocks into soft sand...

Sliding into the vast ocean... "Weee!"

Churning rollercoaster,

in a raging storm!

"Whoa!"

"Ahhh!"

Wild! Giddy!

Rolling ocean waves.

Dancing with the dolphins.

Waltzing with the whales.

My ebb and flow.

Lapping in and out of the shore.

Sliding, sweeping across the sand.

In and out.

Swoosh. Swish. Swoosh.

Floating from sky, to land • to ocean, to sky.

Reflecting, transforming.
Dancing with everything on my path.
Turning rocks into sand.

Author's note

Dear Parent / Grandparent / Adult / Teacher / Child

When I wrote this story, I pictured you and your child creating joyful memories with One Drop as you read this book out loud, together.

As you journey with One Drop, I hope you feel inspired by the words, nature and imagery in this book, exploring the beautiful, illustrated world of One Drop and friends.

Next time you are on a nature walk together, tell us what you see, feel and hear around your local waterways. We would love to see your artwork and the stories you create from your journey.

For more inspiration and a free gift please visit my website: www.01.drop.com.

Jayshree

About the author

Jayshree L Patel, grew up in New Zealand. While she was living in Texas, *One Drop, Endless Ripples* was inspired by the melting ice following the Texas snowstorm in February 2021. This book explores the timeless lessons that nature teaches us about transformation and limitless possibility.

About the illustrator

Alexandra McLellan is a Texas artist with a close New Zealand connection. Her artistic interest in marine biology made her the perfect choice to illustrate this journey of water.

19907973R00020